MOTHER EARTH
AND HER CHILDREN

A Quilted Fairy Tale

Sibylle von Olfers

Illustrated by Sieglinde Schoen Smith

Translated by Jack Zipes

Breckling Press

Library of Congress Cataloging–in–Publication Data
Olfers, Sibylle, 1881–1916.
  [Etwas von den Wurzelkindern. English]
  Mother Earth and her children : a quilted fairy tale / Sibylle von Olfers;
  illustrated by Sieglinde Schoen Smith ; translated by Jack Zipes.
        p. cm.
  Summary: Mother Earth's children, who have been sleeping all winter awake and
experience the new life, the color, and the joys of spring.
  ISBN-13: 978-1-933308-18-0
  ISBN-10: 1-933308-18-4
  [1. Spring--Fiction. 2. Nature--Fiction. 3. Stories in rhyme.] I. Schoen Smith,
Sieglinde, 1941- ill. II. Zipes, Jack David. III. Title.

  PZ8.3.O4655Mo 2007
  [E]--dc22

2007020220

Translated from the original German tale, *Etwas von den Wurzelkindern*

by Sibylle von Olfers, 1906

This book was set in Carlton, Phiastos and Windlass

Editorial direction by Anne Knudsen

Editorial consultant: Helen Knudsen

Cover and interior design by Maria Mann

Photography by Cathy Meals

Fourth Printing, 2008

Published by Breckling Press
283 N. Michigan St, Elmhurst, IL 60126

Printed and bound in China

International Standard Book Number (ISBN 13): 978-1-933308-18-0

International Standard Book Number (ISBN 10): 1-933308-18-4

EDICATION

In memory of Steven

"Wake up, wake up,
My children dear.
Spring is coming,
Spring is near!"

Sleepy children
Open their eyes.
They stretch and yawn
With soft, slow smiles.

YELLOW

BLUE

GREEN

All are quick
And ever ready
To sew spring clothes.
Their hands are steady.

With needles, scissors,
Spools of thread,
They measure and cut,
Full steam ahead.

And when the children's
Clothes are done,
Kind Mother Earth
Admires each one.

Yet since there are
Still chores a-plenty,
They dust and scrub,
No hands are empty.

Brushes and colors,
Are set to go,
To paint the beetles.
See how they glow!

And when fair spring
Arrives on time,
A merry group
Soon comes alive.

Ladybugs, lilies,
Tall blades of grass,
Emerge on the earth
In a joyous mass!

Deep in the woods
All cloaked in green
Flowers blossom.
What a wondrous scene!

A violet hides
Behind a tree,
Scared by a snail,
So strange to see.

Beside the brook
Those earthly tots
Skip among
Forget-me-nots.

They swarm the meadow
Like little bees,
Dance with dandelions
Play among reeds.

Beetles and butterflies
Delight in the day.
If only the summer
Would not fade away.

But autumn comes,
The storm clouds burst,
And rush the tots home
To good Mother Earth.

Now off to bed
My little ones.
Sweet dreams until
The next year comes!"

FROM FAIRY TALE TO QUILT

"Where do all the colors in the flowers come from, Mama?" This was a question of great importance to me when I was a little girl. Mama's answer, "God did it with His magic," did little to satisfy my curiosity. Exactly how did God do it, even if He did use His magic? Were the colors hiding inside green stems and leaves, just waiting for those tight little buds to blossom? I caused my poor mother much distress by digging through bloom after bloom in her much loved garden, destroying many of them as I searched for the colors inside.

I never did find God's paint, nor did I solve the secret to His magic. This remained a mystery to me for many years. Even today, though I understand all the grown-up scientific answers, color, and how we see it, is still a puzzle—or let's say a miracle—to me.

Hello, my name is Sieglinde Schoen Smith. I was born in southern Germany during World War II, the next-to-youngest of five sisters. My sister Hannelore was ten years older than me, and that poor girl often had to babysit me while doing her homework. To keep me quiet, she would let me look at her pretty books. My absolute favorite was *Etwas von den Wurzelkindern*: the same book you are now holding in your hands, though yours is translated from German into English. I loved the pictures and would look at them for hours. Sometimes, if I was a good girl, Hannelore would read the poem aloud. The book became very special to me. You see, I had nothing of my own to play with. When I was growing up in post–war Germany, there simply were no toys or books for children like me.

I came to the United States as a young woman in 1963. Soon I had a family of my own. At bedtime, I would tell my children the story from my favorite book, for I knew the verses by heart, even after so many years had passed. Just a few years ago, during a visit to Germany, I came across a copy of the original book. How happy I was to see those lovely pictures again! At last, I could share them with my children, even though they were grown up now, too.

It was several years later that the story came to mean so much more to me than a child's fairy tale. On July 14, 2002, our much loved son Steven died. I was very unhappy and, even as time passed, my sadness stayed with me. To help keep my mind and my hands busy, a friend suggested I try quilting. Now, my grandmother had lived with us when I was a child, and she was very dear to me. She patiently taught me to sew, among other handcrafting skills. Quilting a few small pieces helped me and brought me some peace during those long nights when I was unable to sleep.

One day, while I was rummaging through my things, looking for ideas for a new quilting project, I came across that little book that had meant so much to me as a child. As I turned the pages, I wondered if those simple paintings might be translated into fabric. I pulled out a pencil and paper and quickly sketched out the drawing in the center pages of the book. It was a lovely image of children coming out of the earth to greet the spring. I turned to my fabrics and got to work. Soon, those curious little characters came alive in my hands. As I sewed, I remembered my own childhood and I thought of my children. In my mind's eye, I saw my own sweet son, Steven.

Once I had recreated the center pages of the book, the quilt took on a life of its own. I began to add images from other parts of the story. Before I knew it, all of the little children, busying themselves with spring tasks and with summer play, were there before me. Still, something was missing.

What should I call the quilt? The original German title of the book, which translates into English as "Something About the Root Children," would never do! To be fair, I did try it out—adding the same heavy black lettering that appeared in the original German picture book. Almost as soon as I finished, I reached for a seam ripper. Off the whole thing came. The words and the letters needed to be as playful as the picture-quilt I had created. So, after a little more doodling, a new title came to me: *Mother Earth and Her Children.*

Since then, the quilt has traveled the country and I have been surprised, and very fortunate, to win much praise and even top honors in two major quilt shows. During one show, I stood back and watched as people stopped to look at my quilt. I realized that the very best part of the quilt is that it seems able to make people smile. When I look at it now, I see my son's sweet smile in the fabric.

A dear lady recently sent me a poem after viewing the quilt. I would like to share it with you.

My Faith is all a doubtful thing
Wove on a doubtful loom,
Until there comes each showery spring.
A cherry tree in bloom.

DAVID MORTON
(American Poet) 1886–1957

ONCE FAMOUS, LONG FORGOTTEN

hen Sibylle von Olfers' *Etwas von den Wurzelkindern*, newly translated as *Mother Earth and Her Children*, first appeared in 1906, nobody could have foreseen its great success. In fact, it has sold more than 800,000 copies over the last one hundred years and has been translated into several different languages. The quaint images in the original book, painted in an art style known as *Jugendstil*, charmed and continue to charm young and old alike. Clearly von Olfers touched a chord in children through her tender poetry and delicate images that still resonate today.

Very little is known about von Olfers, even though *Etwas von den Wurzelkindern* is considered one of the most famous picture books ever published in Germany. She was born in 1881 on her family's estate, the castle of Methgeten, in East Prussia. As was customary in aristocratic families of those times, she received her education at home, and it included art lessons. She displayed an unusual talent for painting and drawing as a teenager, and was sent to Berlin. There, she continued to study art with her aunt, Maria von Olfers, a successful painter and writer. About the time that she published her first book, *What Little Marie Experienced!* (*Was Marilenchen erlebte!*) in 1905, von Olfers decided to join the Catholic order of the sisters of Holy Elizabeth, also known as the "Gray Sisters," and changed her name to Sister Aloysia. After living briefly in Königsberg, she was transferred to Lübeck in northern Germany, where she created *Etwas von den Wurzelkindern* in 1906. The literal translation of the German title is "Something About the Root Children." Clearly, von Olfers wanted to explain to children the roots of the cycle of life by anthropomorphizing nature and by drawing out the close connection between the children and the earth. The anthropomorphological images in her book bring the natural world alive and enable children as readers to identify with it. She also used this style and approach to nature in other picture books that followed, such as *The Little Princess in the Woods* (*Prinzesschen im Wald, 1909*), *Little Wind* (*Windchen, 1910*), and *In the Realm of Butterflies* (*Im Schwetterlingsreich, 1913*). While in Lübeck, von Olfers continued to study at the Art Academy and taught drawing to children in a Catholic elementary school. She had a reputation as a kind and diligent teacher. Unfortunately, soon after World War I erupted in Europe, she died at the very young age of thirty-five due to a lung disease.

Von Olfers began studying art at a time when there were significant changes in approaches toward painting and toward children. By the end of the nineteenth century, educators and artists alike began to focus on the innocence of children rather than treat them as potential sinners in need of discipline. Von Olfers expresses a loving attitude toward children in her works, and she benefited from the new techniques of impressionism and *Jugendstil*. In particular, she was influenced by the works of two well-known illustrators

for children, Ernst Kreidolf and Eva Beskow, whose works featured soft pastel colors, sharp ink drawings, naïve images of children and nature, and rhymed verse. She was also aware of the artwork of such important English illustrators as Walter Crane, Randolph Caldecott, and others who celebrated the innocence of childhood in nature.

What is striking in von Olfers' book is the joy that she conveys through her poetry and images about the rebirth of the world. Under the earth, the children, dressed in brown garments, awake and immediately begin to create clothes for themselves and to adorn the insects that surround them. Once they pass Mother Earth's examination by displaying the sparkling clothes that they have made, there is the full page spread of their colorful march and emergence above the earth. Now they and the insects, dressed in bright colors, flourish and give birth to an idyllic world. Interestingly, there are no adults in this world to control or threaten them. The children are clearly identified with spring and also with the resurgence of natural life. Their exuberant colors and their movements are similar to those of the insects, flowers, grass, and animals. They are curious, sensitive little human beings whose play is in harmony with nature. Only when they are threatened with the coming of autumn and decay do they flee back to Mother Earth, that is, they return to the underground to sleep until they are reborn again.

It is the cycle of birth, life, and death that von Olfers captures with great sensitivity in the metaphorical images and poetic cadence of her book. The children are depicted as the bearers of life and joy. When left alone, they will explore the natural world and rejoice in its wonders, as von Olfers shows. They do not feel threatened, oppressed, or worried. They move in time and in rhythm with nature so that they know when it is time to return home to Mother Earth, who nurtures them so that they will revive and celebrate the rejuvenation of the world each spring.

Though von Olfers was clearly a dedicated religious person, there is not the slightest hint of moral didacticism in her book. On the other hand, there is a reverence for nature that one rarely finds in children's books at the turn of the century. For that matter, it is rare even today to find such a charming picture book for children, one that celebrates their curiosity and imagination while capturing the wondrous world of nature.

Jack Zipes
Professor of German Literature,
University of Minnesota